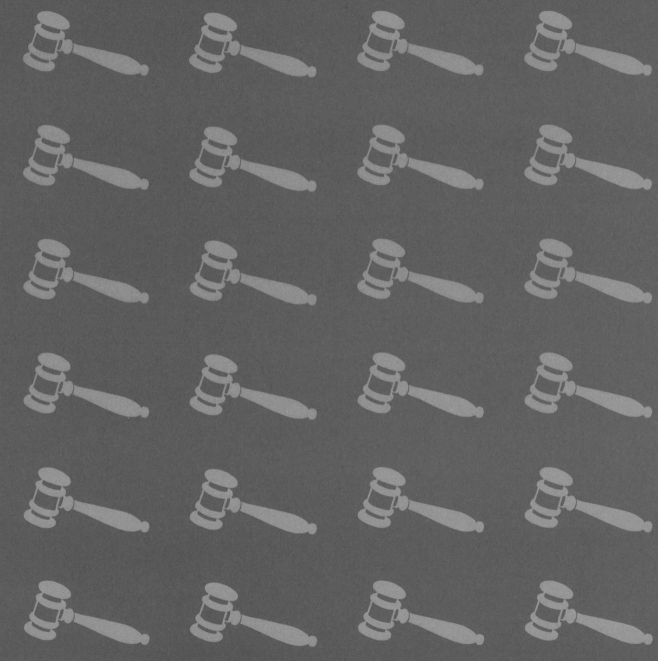

ORDINARY
PEOPLE
CHANGE
the
WORLD

I am
Sonia Sotomayor

BRAD MELTZER

illustrated by Christopher Eliopoulos

 DIAL BOOKS FOR YOUNG READERS

I am **Sonia Sotomayor.**

In Spanish that's *Yo soy Sonia Sotomayor.*

I was born in New York City, and my family came from Puerto Rico.
I learned to speak Spanish before I spoke English.
My family called me Ají—which means *hot pepper*—because I was always jumping around and finding trouble.
My mother used to say...

Even when my mother or my abuelita—my grandmother—dressed me up, my clothes would get wrinkled. Ribbons never stayed in my hair.

One time, I got my head stuck in a bucket while I was trying to hear what my voice sounded like inside.

SONIA, WHAT HAVE YOU DONE NOW?

HELLLOOOOOOO IN THERE!

I also loved making up games, jousting like a knight with my little brother on my back.

CHARGE!

CRASH!

SONIA, WHAT HAVE YOU DONE NOW?

One of my favorite places was my abuelita's apartment.
Entering her home was like going straight to Puerto Rico.
Once a month at Abuelita's, my mom and my aunts would make sofrito, a spicy sauce.
As they chopped peppers, onions, and tomatoes, I'd sneak to eat them right out of the blender.

The grown-ups played lots of music—
and games too, like dominoes.

One of my favorite moments was when everyone would go quiet and my abuelita would perform for us. She looked so glamorous. We'd all be mesmerized as she read one of her favorite Puerto Rican poems by José Gautier Benitez.

I understood what the poem meant.
I had so many dreams.

When I was little, I used to imagine myself as the hero of my favorite book series—Nancy Drew, girl detective.

Nancy was a master at doing puzzles, and no matter what got in her way, she could figure things out.

She lived in a big house and solved crimes with her dad. Since he was a lawyer, he'd give her the best hints.

In my neighborhood, dreams like that rarely came true.
There weren't any detectives who looked like me.

We didn't live in a fancy house. We lived in a small apartment.
My mother was a nurse, so I knew some Puerto Rican nurses. But
there was only one Puerto Rican doctor.

At the stores where we shopped, there were a lot of Puerto Rican
workers, but few managers or owners, and even fewer lawyers and
detectives.

It wasn't that my Puerto Rican neighbors didn't work hard.
People aren't poor because they're lazy.
My mother worked long hours to pay our bills.
But sometimes where you live affects the kind of
opportunities you have.

My mom worked extra hours so she could pay to send my brother
and me to a more respected school, where we'd get a better education.
But even with a good school, my young life was still pretty
complicated.

When I was nine years old, I was diagnosed with diabetes, a disease that means your body keeps too much sugar in your blood.

I was strong. I could handle the shot.

Something even harder happened later that year.
My father died.
It was like an earthquake in my life. My world started to change and felt scary.
One of the ways I found comfort was doing what you're doing right now: reading.
I loved books.

In that book, I learned that my name was a version of Sophia, meaning *wisdom*.

Those days were hard for my mom.
She had to pay for two kids all by herself, but it didn't slow her down.
She ordered us a full set of the Encyclopedia Britannica.
When it arrived, it was like an early Christmas.

Each book was so heavy. It was like we lived in a library.
The books were expensive too—my mom struggled to make
the payments.
But with the encyclopedia, the world expanded before me
in a thousand new directions.

There was another reason why my world continued to change: my teachers.

Every teacher has the power to inspire us kids.

This one realized I loved to compete and win.

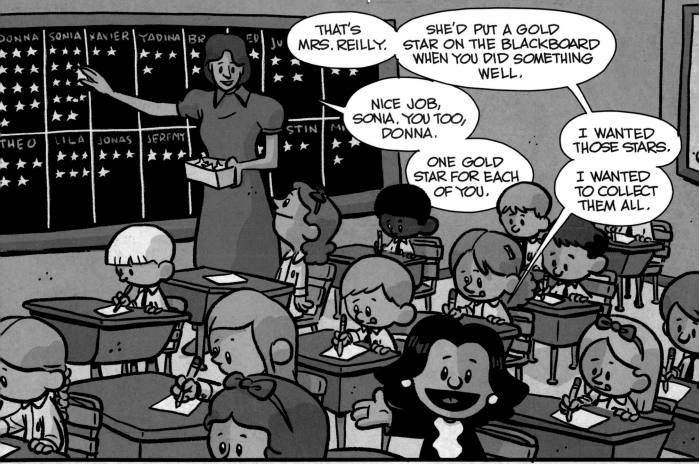

The first time I got an A grade on my report card, I made a promise to myself: I would add one more A each time.

With grades like that, I was on my way to becoming a detective.

Did that mean everything was suddenly easy?

Not in my neighborhood.

Where we lived, if you didn't lock up your bike, it usually got stolen.

And if you walked down the wrong alley, someone might try to beat you up.

Once, I found my little brother surrounded by bullies, so I walked over to protect him.

That didn't mean I couldn't be hurt.

One day, I was reading about diabetes. It said that people with diabetes, like me, could be a doctor, a lawyer, an engineer, even a teacher.

But because of my disease...

YOU CAN BE... DOCTOR LAWYER ... WRITER COOK MAIL CARRIER

YOU CAN'T BE... A POLICE OFFICER

WHAT?!

If I couldn't be a police officer, I couldn't be a detective—which meant I couldn't be like Nancy Drew!

I was devastated—but I wasn't defeated.
I quickly found a new role model on a TV show.
He was a lawyer named Perry Mason.
He used his smarts in the courtroom to figure out
the truth behind each crime.

Perry Mason was definitely the hero of the show,
but I was more fascinated by a different character...

The judge.
Every episode, no matter what Perry Mason was trying to do, it was the judge who made the final decision.

It was hard to understand every detail.
But I could tell that each case was like a good puzzle—a complicated game with its own rules.
From there, I knew I could be a great lawyer—even a great judge.

To be a judge, I had to learn to speak in front of others.

My first practice session was in church, doing a Bible reading.

GOOD SPEAKERS HAVE TO LOOK AT PEOPLE AND MAKE EYE CONTACT.

BUT I WAS SO NERVOUS, I USED THIS TRICK:

I STARED AT PEOPLE'S FOREHEADS INSTEAD.

THEY HAD NO IDEA.

I did it. And I knew I could do it again.

In high school, I joined forensics, which trains you in public speaking and debate.

I won first prize in a speaking contest. But I also learned that one of the most important parts of making a good argument is being a good listener. My talk was about how we have a responsibility to look out for each other.

Yet, perhaps the best thing I learned in forensics came from one of the student coaches.

A counselor at school had told me to apply to a local college. But the coach told me I could go farther.

It sounded impossible.
I didn't think kids from the South Bronx could go to fancy schools like Princeton.

But like my abuelita's poem said, to get what you want, you must dream it.

I was valedictorian of my high school class. But would they accept me?

Princeton seemed like a different planet.
Most of the kids here came from wealthy neighborhoods and fancy schools.
They were used to skiing trips, tennis lessons, and vacations in Europe.
I'd barely ever left the Bronx.

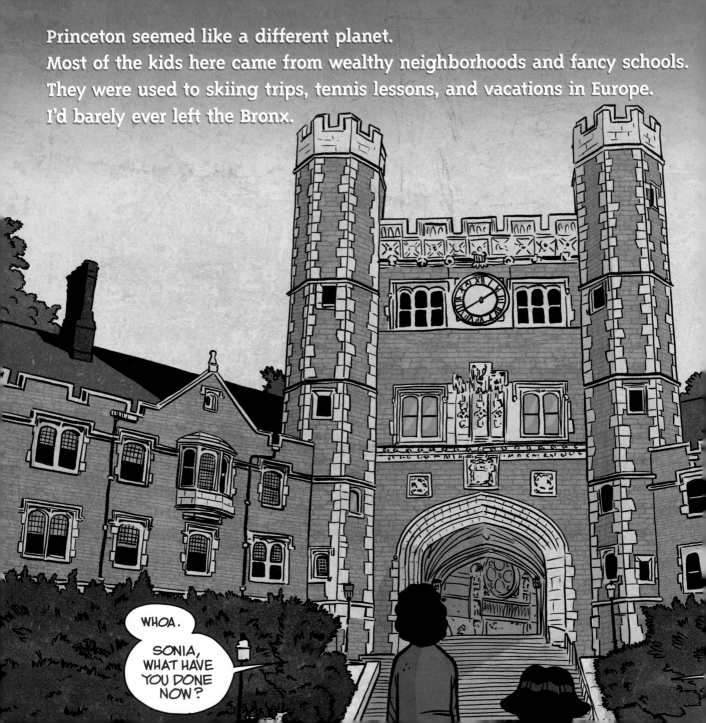

I'M NOT EXACTLY SURE, MAMI.

That first week at college, I couldn't sleep because I heard a cricket in my room.

SONIA, IT'S NOT IN YOUR ROOM.

IT'S OUTSIDE, ON THE TREE.

In New York, we didn't have trees outside our windows.

Even though I got really homesick, I again found that books made me feel better.

Here in the Firestone Library, I saw just how much knowledge there was in the world.

During my time at Princeton, I did so well, they invited me into Phi Beta Kappa, an honor society that recognizes top students.

I almost threw away the invitation, thinking it was a fake-jewelry scam.

I'd never heard of any of the awards they gave me, including the Pyne Prize, the most prestigious award a Princeton senior can win.

To some people, athletes or astronauts are heroes.

To me, the best action hero was a lawyer.

That's what I wanted to be.

So after graduation, I went to Yale Law, the top law school in the country.

During my third year at law school, I walked by a meeting that was offering free snacks.

I was a bit hungry, so I stepped inside, stumbling into a presentation that would change my life.

Inspired by my old dreams, I became an assistant district attorney.

As a prosecutor, my job was to find the truth—and to make sure that if someone committed a crime, they didn't get away with it.

When I started, there were so few Hispanic and female prosecutors, the other lawyers would ask me...

It didn't stop me from doing my job.

I just had to convince the jury to agree with me.

I also understood that when people don't get along, it's usually because they can't imagine how someone else is feeling.

From there, I had a few different jobs as a lawyer.
Until one day, I heard that the U.S. District Court in Manhattan was looking for...

My boss was so determined, he put the application on my desk and made sure I had no other work that would get in the way of it.

This was my dream, wasn't it?

Of course it was. And it was coming true.

I became the city's first Hispanic federal judge—and its youngest as well.

Now my job was to make sure that in each case, people followed the laws correctly.

During my very first trial, I was so nervous, my knees were actually knocking.

Once the case got started, my panic passed.
I was ready to do my job—and also ready for what was
coming next when I was promoted to the Court of Appeals.

Soon, I was considered for the biggest legal job of all, being a Justice on the Supreme Court of the United States.

That's the court where the most important cases are decided—the Justices are the ones who make those decisions.

I was worried that the job would change my life, but a friend told me...

It made me think about the South Bronx. It made me think that there were no Hispanic female lawyers for me to follow at Princeton, Yale, the District Attorney's Office, or even as a judge. It made me think about all of the people I could inspire.

I needed to show them it was possible.

On October 8, 2009, at 55 years old, I was sworn in as the first Hispanic and third female Justice to ever serve on the Supreme Court of the United States.

In my life, I was the Ají.
The hot pepper.
The one who wouldn't slow down.
Because of where I was from—because I was poor and Latina—some people didn't think I would go far.
But there were others who helped my dreams come to life.
They gave me opportunities and reminded me to keep going.

Those are the people you need to listen to.
Pay attention to the ones who believe in you.
The more you learn, the farther you'll go.
Education is a rocket ship.
It can take you anywhere.
But no matter how high you fly...

Whether it's in English, Spanish, or any other language, our dreams are often the same:
A loving family.
Kind friends.
A safe place to call home.
And the chance to reach our potential.

The world outside your window is a starting point. But there's so much more beyond that. Read. Study. Do right by people.

No matter where you're born, there's no limit to what you can accomplish.

I am Sonia Sotomayor. *Yo soy Sonia Sotomayor.*

I am proof that with opportunity comes justice.

"*Remember that no one succeeds alone.*"
—Sonia Sotomayor

Timeline

JUNE 25, 1954	1963	1972	1976
Born in New York City	Is diagnosed with diabetes	Graduates as valedictorian of Cardinal Spellman High School in the Bronx, NY	Graduates from Princeton University

Sonia, with her brother
and mother, being sworn
in as a Supreme Court Justice

Sonia as a
Princeton student

The U.S. Supreme
Court Justices, 2018

1976	1979	1992	1998	AUGUST 8, 2009
Marries Kevin Noonan (they divorce 7 years later)	Graduates from Yale Law School	Becomes U.S. District Court Judge	Becomes U.S. Court of Appeals Judge	Sworn in as first Hispanic Supreme Court Justice of the U.S.

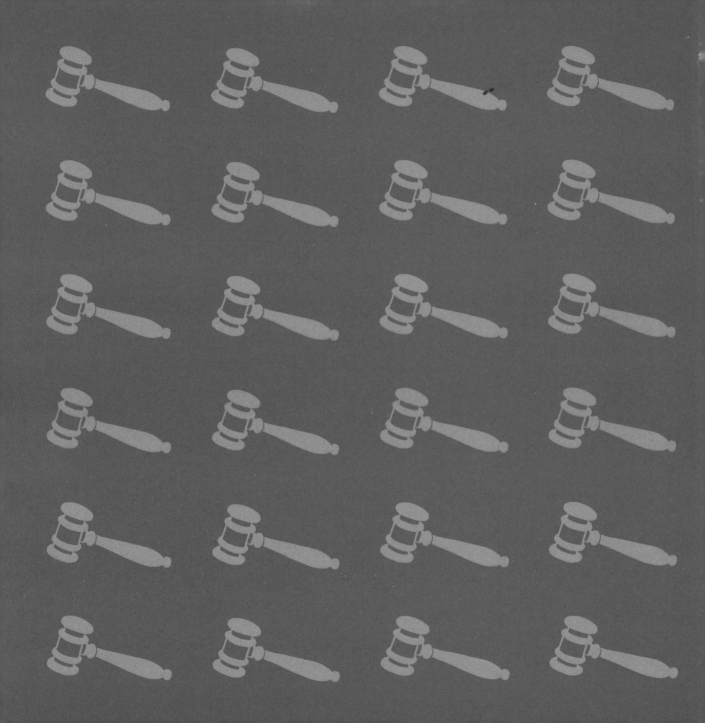